The Comical Cockerel

Heidi Villiers & Marjorie Ouvry

There was a pretty Scottish House,
Folks called it, "The Old Manse"
And all the pets, who lived there, dreamt
That they could **sing** and **dance**!

By day they were contented
In their hutches, coop and cage

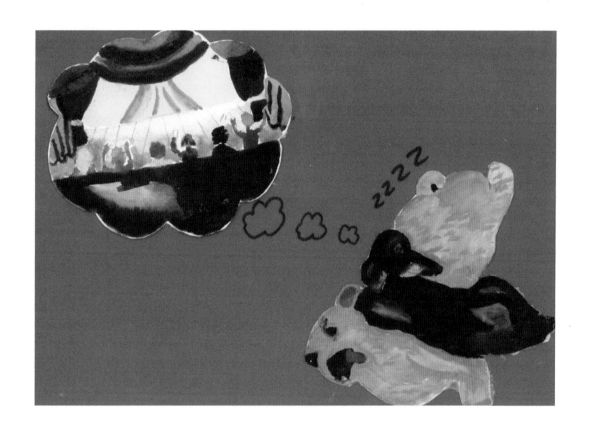

By night, some creatures dreamt that
They performed, upon the **stage**!

One morning **VERY** early
The Cock-er-el named **Rick**,
Decided, very naughtily,
That he would play a trick

Earlier than usual
Rick crowed with all his might
And all his friends were **very** cross
To leave their dreams of night

"Cock-A-Doodle-Doo!" cries Rick
With crimson wobbling chin,
The hen with feathered feet complains,
"Who's making such a din?"

'I dreamt I was...

"Cock-A-Doodle-Doo!" crows Rick
With shiny feathers bright.

Two yawning budgies now complain,
"You gave us such a fright,
We dreamt we were...

... the King and Queen who dine by candlelight!"

"Cock-A-Doodle-Doo!!" Please Rick
I'm **begging** you to stop it.
The fluffy guinea pig complains,
"You're making such a racket!

I dreamt I was...

...a gangster in a double-breasted jacket!

"Cock-A-Doodle-Doo!" squawks Rick,
"Your crowing's such a hassle'
The tube-shaped sausage dog complains,
You noisy, feathered rascal!

I dreamt I was...

... A piper at Auld Edinburgh Castle.

"Cock-A-Doodle-D !" laughs Rick
"A lazy bunch you are."

The tiny, big eared mouse complains,
"I heard you from afar,

I dreamt I was...

... a singer

Yes, a famous op'ra star!

"Cock-A-Doodle-Doo!", Rick shrieks,
(The noisiest of pets)

The goldfish in the pond complain,
'Oh, is it morning yet ?'
We dreamt...

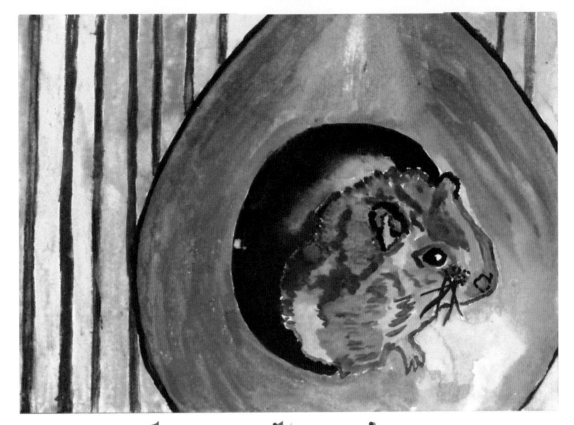

"Cock-A-Doodle-Doo!", Rick shouts
his orders like a Colonel,
The hamster, bleary eyed, complains,
"That crowing is infernal!
Does he not know that some of us,
Who live here, are nocturnal?"

"Cock-A-Doodle-Doo!" Rick crows

Great trees of copper beech!

The squirrel from his tree complains

Why does he always screech?

I dreamt I'd found an acorn that was juicy as a peach!

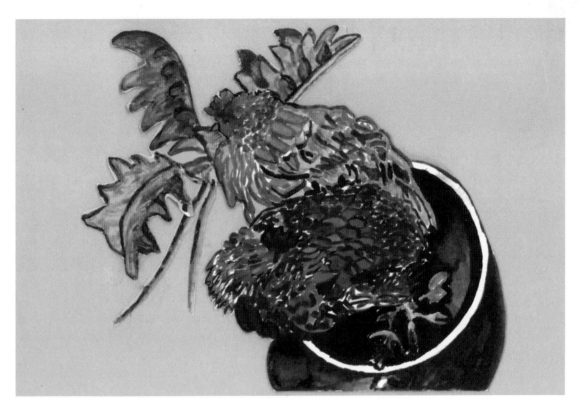

Next morn, **Rick** played **another** joke.
This time he did NOT crow.
"What time is it?" the chickens asked,
"Without **Rick** we don't know!
I hope we get our morning food
If not, we will not grow!"

And soon the hens began to cluck,
The mouse began to **squeak**,
The budgies on their perch went "Tweet!
We've **nothing** here to eat!"
How can we wake the children up
If Rick is still asleep?

Then "Cock-A-Doodle-Doo!", arose
From cheeky, roguish **Rick**.
The children woke and fed the pets.
It was a **splendid** trick!

"You've me to thank for waking up
The children, so you're fed!"

So **three cheers** for a wake-up call,

Instead of **dreams** in bed!

This book is dedicated to the following pets...

ROZIE THE DACHSHUND

BALFIE THE SQUIRREL

BUTTERCUP HEN

BETSY AND LADY ANNE BANTAMS

CHI CHI THE HAMSTER

FINGAL AND SHERBERT BUDGIES

CLEOPATRA AND AUDREY GUINEA PIGS

For you to draw your own pets' dreams...

For you to draw your own pets' dreams...

For you to draw your own pets' dreams...

Printed in Great Britain
by Amazon